P9-BYJ-655

THE BOY WHO DIDN'T BELIEVE IN SPRING

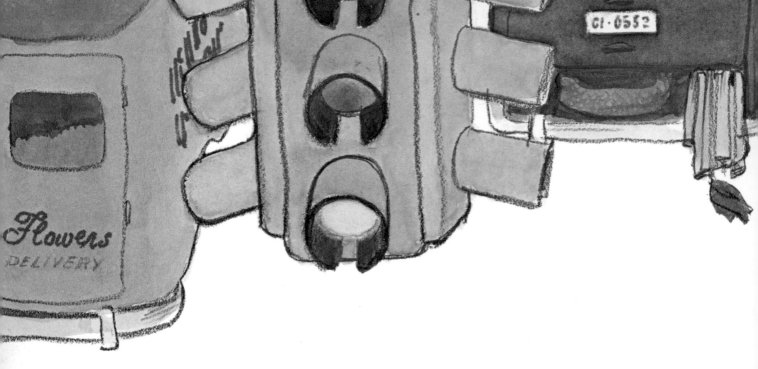

THE BOY WHO DIDN'T

LUCILLE CLIFTON

BELIEVE IN SPRING

pictures by BRINTON TURKLE

A PUFFIN UNICORN

Text copyright © 1973 by Lucille Clifton
Illustrations copyright © 1973 by Brinton Turkle

All rights reserved.

Unicorn is a registered trademark of E. P. Dutton

Library of Congress number 87-27145
ISBN 0-14-054739-8

Published in the United States by
Dutton Children's Books,
a member of Penguin Putnam Inc.
375 Hudson Street, New York, New York 10014

Editor: Ann Durell   Designer: Hilda Scott

Printed in Hong Kong by South China Printing Co.
First Unicorn Edition 1988
20   19   18   17   16   15   14

For Shawnie

Once upon a time there was a little boy named
King Shabazz who didn't believe in Spring.

"No such thing!" he would whisper every
time the teacher talked about Spring in school.

"Where is it at?" he would holler every time his Mama
talked about Spring at home.

He used to sit with his friend Tony Polito on the bottom
step when the days started getting longer and warmer and
talk about it.

"Everybody talkin bout Spring!" he would say to Tony.

"Big deal," Tony would say back.

"No such thing!" he would say to Tony.

"Right!" Tony would say back.

One day after the teacher had been talking about birds that were blue and his Mama had started talking about crops coming up, King Shabazz decided he had just had enough. He put his jacket on and his shades and went by for Tony Polito.

"Look here, man," King said when they got out to the bottom step, "I'm goin to get me some of this Spring."

"What you mean, man?" Tony asked him.

"Everybody talkin bout Spring comin, and Spring just round the corner. I'm goin to go round there and see what do I see."

Tony Polito watched King Shabazz get up and push his shades up tight on his nose.

"You comin with me, man?" he said while he was pushing.

Tony Polito thought about it for a minute. Then he got up and turned his cap around backwards.

"Right!" Tony Polito said back.

King Shabazz and Tony Polito had been around the
corner before, but only as far as the streetlight alone.

They passed the school and the playground.

"Ain't no Spring in there," said King Shabazz with a laugh. "Sure ain't," agreed Tony Polito.

They passed Weissman's. They stopped for a minute by
the side door at Weissman's and smelled the buns.

"Sure do smell good," whispered Tony.

"But it ain't Spring," King was quick to answer.

They passed the apartments and walked fast in case they met Junior Williams. He had said in school that he was going to beat them both up.

Then they were at the streetlight. Tony stopped and made believe his sneaker was untied to see what King was going to do. King stopped and blew on his shades to clean them and to see what Tony was going to do. They stood there for two light turns and then King Shabazz grinned at Tony Polito, and he grinned back, and the two boys ran across the street.

"Well, if we find it, it ought to be now," said King.

Tony didn't say anything. He just stood looking around.
"Well, come on, man," King whispered, and they started
down the street.

They passed the Church of the Solid Rock with high
windows all decorated and pretty.

They passed a restaurant with little round tables near the window. They came to a take-out shop and stood by the door a minute to smell the bar-b-q.

"Sure would like to have some of that," whispered King.

"Me too," whispered Tony with his eyes closed. They
walked slower down the street.

Just after they passed some apartments King Shabazz and Tony Polito came to a vacant lot. It was small and had high walls from apartments on three sides of it. Three walls around it and right in the middle—a car!

It was beautiful. The wheels were gone and so were the doors, but it was dark red and sitting high on a dirt mound in the middle of the lot.

"Oh man, oh man," whispered King.

"Oh man," whispered Tony.

Then they heard the noise.

It was a little long sound, like smooth things rubbing against rough, and it was coming from the car. It happened again. King looked at Tony and grabbed his hand.

"Let's see what it is, man," he whispered. He thought Tony would say no and let's go home. Tony looked at King and held his hand tightly.

"Right," he said very slowly.

The boys stood there a minute, then began tiptoeing over toward the car. They walked very slowly across the lot. When they were halfway to the car, Tony tripped and almost fell. He looked down and saw a patch of little yellow pointy flowers, growing in the middle of short spiky green leaves.

"Man, I think you tripped on these crops!" King laughed.

"They're comin up," Tony shouted. "Man, the crops are comin up!"

And just as Tony was making all that noise, they heard another noise, like a lot of things waving in the air, and they looked over at the car and three birds flew out of one of the door holes and up to the wall of the apartment.

King and Tony ran over to the car to see where the birds had been. They had to climb up a little to get to the door and look in.

They stood there looking a long time without saying anything. There on the front seat down in a whole lot of cottony stuff was a nest. There in the nest were four light blue eggs. Blue. King took off his shades.

"Man, it's Spring," he said almost to himself.

"Anthony Polito!"

King and Tony jumped down off the mound. Some-body was shouting for Tony as loud as he could.

"Anthony Polito!"

The boys turned and started walking out of the vacant lot. Tony's brother Sam was standing at the edge of the lot looking mad.

"Ma's gonna kill you, after I get finished, you squirt!" he hollered.

King Shabazz looked at Tony Polito and took his hand.

"Spring is here," he whispered to Tony.

"Right," whispered Tony Polito back.

LUCILLE CLIFTON was the Discovery Winner at the YMHA Poetry Center in New York City in 1969 and was named Poet Laureate of Maryland in 1979. Her many books for children include *My Friend Jacob* and *Amifika*. Born in Depew, New York, Mrs. Clifton spent most of her childhood in Buffalo. She attended Howard University and Fredonia State College. The mother of six, she currently lives in Santa Cruz, California.

BRINTON TURKLE is the well-known author-illustrator of *Deep in the Forest* (an ALA Notable Book); *Do Not Open*; *Thy Friend, Obadiah* (a Caldecott Honor Book); and other books about Obadiah, a young Quaker boy in Nantucket. Mr. Turkle says *The Boy Who Didn't Believe in Spring* was a "fresh challenge," requiring as much research as some of his historical books. "I had to study many things I'd always taken for granted or ignored. *The Boy Who Didn't Believe in Spring* helped me rediscover New York—sketching boys' jackets, tennis shoes, buses, traffic lights, street signs."